The Lion and the Saint

A NOVELLA

Laura E. Wolfe

ANCIENT FAITH PUBLISHING

CHESTERTON, INDIANA

Published by:
   Ancient Faith Publishing
   A Division of Ancient Faith Ministries
   P.O. Box 748
   Chesterton, IN 46304

ISBN: 978-1-944967-82-6

Library of Congress Control Number: 2020944460

For my dad, who believes in me.
Love you.

Contents

King

AM MAJESTY. I am lord. This is the way it is written in the book of life. I cannot be other than what I am; I was not made a mouse to mewl at sand cats and shy at shadows. I am the king of beasts, and a king does not bow and scrape to the rabble. I am lion, venerable regent of desert and savanna both. I know no fear.

In the whole of this land I rule without rival; the bones of my challengers now lie bleaching in the sun. Yet once upon a time I was a princeling, the sole cub nursed and gentled by my mother, the leading lioness of a large and healthy pride. My earliest memories are an endless golden afternoon of wrestling games with my kitten-ish cousins and the playful pawing of the tufted ears of my patient aunts. There is a timelessness to youth, peace that blurs into eternity, even if it can be counted in weeks or months. No one remembers its beginning, and none ever forgets its end.

In our tradition, it is the lionesses who teach the cubs what it means to be lion, whispering the rules and secrets of our nature into our baby-round ears. I suppose that for the females this process never ends, but of their hidden ways I know nothing. Male cubs must learn quickly, for our time uncontested in the pride is measured in so few short years. Then come the lessons of solitude that we teach ourselves. But cubs do not think of solitude—in the golden morning of life, joy and togetherness are what it means to be lion.

Then came the day when, to test my growing strength, I dared to stalk my visiting sire as he napped in the grass. My eyes were bright, my muscles smooth and primed with the vigor of fresh meat. Even my whiskers did not twitch against my will. Confident of my blossoming skill, I crept in the shade of a cloud shadow, the rumor of a *khamaseen* breeze licking at my face, blowing my scent off to the river. I chose the moment of every footfall, and when I pounced on his tawny tail, my sire was unprepared and provoked to rage. He would have slain me then but for the intercession of my lioness mother, who leaped between us and snarled in warning. She was a magnificent cat, my mother, her lean muscles rippling like steppe grass under a coat that shone like sunbeams. Many males had perished vying for the right to her bloodline. Even so, my sire swatted at her gleaming topaz eyes before he turned and stalked away.

That was the end of my time with the pride. As if the land itself were in concord with the fury of my father, the khamaseen gales whipped into an eye-scouring frenzy and buffeted the grasses and the groves. All life took shelter, and when the wild winds of the sandstorm had passed, twilight painted the dome of the world in blood-orange and platinum. In the quiet after the storm, my mother and aunts gathered around me, caressing me with their soft muzzles and murmuring sounds of tenderness and fare-well. My kittenish girl-cousins, grown into slender maidens nearly blooming, demurely turned their gazes towards the setting sun.

I stood on the border of my home territory, and the wind ruffled the wisps of my new mane. I am lion, I know no fear—but at that moment I knew my first loneliness, profound and deep as the sea of which my lioness aunts had rumbled stories. With nothing better to do, I journeyed to the east in search of the great water that would mirror and soothe the vast echoing chamber of my heart.

I walked and slept, hunted and ate. The moon

chased the sun across the sky, veiling and revealing her pale gaze. I had no words then with which to tell my story—they came later—and time without words rolls along like the great river, the Now always present, always moving.

Two moon's journeys away from home, I met my older brother.

He was the cub of a litter from three summers before me, a full-blooded sibling by both my mother and my sire. I did not know him as a cub, but the story of his banishment was still fresh in the pride's memory, still prickly with shame against my mother's honor. Unlike me, he did not challenge our sire at the brink of his maturity. One night he left the pride on a solitary hunt; he returned in the morning stinking of strange blood. It is said that he offered a piece of manflesh in tribute to our sire, who roared in disapproval and slashed at the face of my brother. Our sire would have slain him them, for a maneater wrongs the earth where he walks and is less than he was meant to be, and my lioness mother would not have argued against the act. But my brother was fast and vicious as only a maneater can be, and he mauled the ear of my sire before beating a hasty retreat to the desert.

I marked the edge of his territory by its sudden rankness; even the bending of the grasses and the shadows of the clouds seemed tainted by the scent that was almost familiar, nearly kin, but rotten. I am lion, I know no fear—but I do not disdain caution, for life is preferable to a foolish death. I stalked quietly through the scrub, my ears pricked for a misplaced sigh of grass.

He thought to surprise me from behind. Fool.

For I am the scion of my lioness mother, seed of my noble sire, unmarred by any wrongness that is contrary to my nature. I felt him stalking the moment he laid eyes on me—I marked him tracking me for some distance before his attack. When he finally decided to pounce, I met him mid-air with the earth-shaking power of my first roar.

My lion's heart pounded with the adrenaline of my premiere fight, and though he was strong, he was no match for the zeal of my youth. I seized his throat in my jaws and laid him low on the grass, his blood an offering for his sins against the land. The wind lifted his spirit from his flesh, lifting also the darkness from his territory.

I sat back on my haunches and roared again in victory. My brother's territory—my territory—hushed, making its first obeisance.

The trill of a baboon broke the silence. I turned to find her, hidden in the scrub and peering cautiously from behind a branch.

I give you thanks, my lord, she hooted, and her sounds had meaning beyond a baboon's mere instinct and reaction. I did not understand it then, but out of the darkness of the temple she brought me words, and the words she offered gave shape to my thoughts.

Who is it that addresses me? I growled haughtily.

Just a hamadryas, my lord. Her musical voice

played treble to the deepening baritone of my rumblings.

Where is your troop? Who leads you? I asked her in the animal manner, as if communicating with a fellow lion. To my astonishment, she answered me both in animal gesture and in those drops of light that were her words. That I understood those words surprised her, but I am lion and capable of many magnificent deeds.

There is no one else, my lord. Only I, alone. The maneater has consumed many in his insatiable hunger, and the rest have escaped to other lands.

Alone. Hearing it spoken, I felt the prick of it anew. *Why do you remain alone?* I wondered.

I am a solitary baboon, she answered, *taken from my band as an infant and raised as a temple monkey by men who preserve the worship of the ibis-headed god, the thrice-great. The maneater devoured their priests and fouled their temple. The sanctuary is abandoned, its worship forsaken, and I am alone.*

I considered this, and offered a simple solution. *I shall eat you, then.*

The baboon could not suppress the shudder that ran from tip to tail. *If you wish, lord. But I would rather you not.*

I snorted. *What would you rather, hamadryas?*

I would follow you, lord. I was raised on the knee of a storyteller, one who sang me the songs of his people and taught me their rhythms and rhymes. With words I would write your epic, lord; I would be the court scribe of the heir of Maahes, just as my namesake Astennu serves Thoth his father, thrice-great and wise, as his companion and clerk.

I know not what to make of your words. I scoffed, my whiskers twitching in annoyance.

The baboon looked down at the ground and traced lines in the dirt. After a moment she looked up, and the words she spoke then would follow me to the end of my days.

It is the legacy of holy men, lord. They make us more than what we are.

Unheard of in the stories of my lioness aunts, for a lion to hold court with a baboon, yet the idea appealed to me. This lowly creature desired to add to my stature and nobility, and I warmed to the stroking of my pride. I dipped my head in acquiescence to her proposal. Besides, I could always eat her later.

And so did my brief reign as king begin.

My mane was not yet full grown the day I began my conquest; but until the day of my abdication there was no beast alive that contested my rights. I am lion, and I am king.

TWO

Scribe

MY LORD HOLDS court in the shade of an olive tree while the sun laves him in worship, imparting gold to gold and warming the pads of his paws. He regards the winds shifting the dunes in the desert distance, noble and impassive. My lord king has redeemed the land of his brother, and all of her inhabitants love him for it.

In the days and moons after the sacrifice of the maneater, my lord king makes good on his regal promises. He scopes out the borders of his territory and presses against the ranges of other solitary males. None shy from confrontation, and those who choose battle against my lord over exile choose also the manner of their own demise. It is a good death for a lone lion, to be conquered by a beast as noble and golden as my lord king. He is swift and merciful.

But is this the right way to begin my part of the story? It is certainly how the lion would want me to begin, with regal language that calls the hearer to the worship of his noble self. It is how the lion thinks, and so it is true as far as it goes, but it is by no means the only layer.

The temple man in the house of Thoth would instruct me to begin with the old story that frames the new like the silver setting around a ruby. He would have me tell of Maahes, the lion-headed god, the warrior who struggles against the serpent, the true protector, over-flowing with strength and power and loyalty.

He would have me remind you of the judgment of Osiris, who weighs the hearts of all against the lightness of a feather, and of Astennu the baboon, who witnesses the tipping of the scale and writes what he sees for all to read for ever and ever.

This is also true as far as it goes, but by no means the only layer. Nor is it the only setting for this jewel, for there are other stories, perhaps as old as the stars and more true than the ones I have been taught.

Enough of this. I am now a scribe, so I shall tell you what happens next, and leave it for you to decide whether I tell it true.

The lion and I travel together for many moons, marking the circle of the seasons. His mane grows thick and tawny with victory as he claims the land for his own. As we travel, words grow between us—funny, spindly little things that try to be more than they are. Soon the time comes for my lord king to take a pride.

The lion would have me tell you that all of the beasts of the land love him, and many rush to do his bidding. I can assure you that though

gratitude for the defeat of the maneater cre-
ated a somewhat peaceable kingdom, prey are
still wary of predators, and the natural order
of things is not overthrown. Most beasts have
never heeded the call of a lion before, and they
obey his haughty wishes in fear more than in
love—though the wild felines of all kinds seem
to all be swept up into the pageantry of the
new king, as if royalty rubs off from one cat to
another.

When his majesty sends forth the decree of
his desire, it is the sand cats, those desert kittens of deceptive softness, who scout the earth
for the scent of lioness. The caracals and genets
who flank us in a darting entourage spread the
message of our quest to all of the creatures
who cower under bushes. We travel mostly in
silence, our feline company weaving in and out
of the shrubs, announcing royal presence to all
who live and breathe. Most of the small creatures chatter in submission before skittering
into the brush, though the spiny hedgehogs curl

into funny little balls and merely wait for us to pass them by. Herds of ibex and oryx dip their striking horns in recognition, though they keep their distance from our troop of carnivores. Our travel is crepuscular, and we rest in the heat of the arid days and the dark of the moonless nights.

So goes his royal progress, which presses the borders of his territory further than ever before. We find no trace of other baboons.

My lord does not speak often, but when he does, he creates himself with the words that grow between us.

"Hamadryas?"

"Yes, my lord?"

"You do not call yourself hamadryas."

"No, my lord." I dip my head humbly, a gesture that pleases him.

"Why not?"

"I was given a name, my lord."

"What is a name?"

I must stop and think on this. Raised by

temple men, I forget that their words do not always fit easily into bodies that speak and hear with growls and fluting.

"A name is a man-word that is only for one. It marks me as not simply hamadryas, but a particular hamadryas."

"Why should you be particular? Isn't it enough to be hamadryas?" The lion sounds vexed.

"Perhaps, lord, it would be enough if I had never known it differently."

He is quiet for a time.

"I am lion. I do not know what it is to be particular."

I nod my head and wait for him to continue.

"Lion is different from lion, but all are lion. Unless they are like my brother, who was less than lion." I do not smile in my amusement at his clumsy thoughts, for I do not wish to provoke him into eating me.

But I do ask him, "If one can be less than a lion, can one be more than a lion, my lord?"

He sneezes quietly in frustration. Lions are kings and not philosophers, after all.

"My lioness mother and her pride were full of what it means to be lion. I never heard them speak of being more."

I shrug. Lions are not known for their oratory, and I am not surprised.

"There is . . . a lion's secret, though. I will tell you now, but if you misuse it, I will eat you."

Danger thrills down my spine to the tip of my nimble tail. It is a sudden change in the tenor of our conversation, and my lord king becomes more than just a questioner.

"Betrayal is not in my nature, lord. I will guard your mysteries," I promise, with a flutter of my heart.

"Pah! I am lion, I do not know mystery. It is hidden because it is regal, and not for the small creatures to know and imagine us soft."

He paws the earth lightly.

"It is commonly known that a lion does not purr like a common sand cat. Such a thing would be beneath us, and our throats are not designed for such vulgarity. But it is not true that we cannot purr at all, though many lions never do. My lioness mother whispered to me the legend that a lion's purr will only reveal itself when one has found his own lionheart. That is the extent of my knowledge. If there is more to the secret, she either did not know or did not tell me."

"But what is a lionheart, my lord?"

A growl rises menacingly from his throat. I have overstepped, and my baboon heart races in the presence of the mighty predator. Fear and fascination compete within me, and though I do not truly think that he will eat me just now, I cannot convince my instincts that this is so.

"I know not," he snarls, and paces away from me.

The dismissal dismays me, for I do not wish the conversation to end, and I am loth to be sent away to keep company with the wordless caracals. Even if I wished to make my own way in the world, I find that each passing day binds me more closely to the presence of my lord, the lion. Where could I go, a solitary, particular hamadryas? What band would have me now that I play at being more than a baboon? Now that I converse with a lion, and tell the stories of men?

It is days before he speaks to me again.

"Hamadryas?" he calls over his golden shoulder. Having followed in the rear, I now scamper to his side.

"Yes, my lord?"

"What is your name?"

It is a peace offering; one that I gratefully accept.

"The temple men called me Astennu, lord."

"What does it mean, hamadryas?"

"I am named for their god, who takes the form of a hamadryas."

"What is a god?"

"It is what they call the voice that whispers to us what we are. They seek its power to grant them wisdom and favorable seasons."

"Astennu." He rolls the word around his

mouth, clicking against his massive canines. "Sharing a name—does it change you? Are you now the god of which they speak?"

I shiver with the implication. I barely know what it means to be a hamadryas—how could I know what it means to be a god? But I do not understand the rules that men make for such things, so I must answer honestly.

"I do not think so, my lord. But I am not certain."

He yawns then, his mouth a great gaping wound in his soft face. His tongue flexes with the force of it, curling and releasing, sliding over his teeth. I tremble in anticipation of his next question, when suddenly his nose darts to the earth, and he whuffs and nuzzles the grass before him.

I smell a female. He has reverted to animal speak, that confluence of body movement and breath that conveys meaning without words.

I drop back a few paces behind him and watch. If I was Astennu to him just a moment ago, now I can be nothing but baboon.

His massive muscles tense and ripple as he springs into a graceful, loping stride. The caracals and genets scatter—they have no pretensions of welcome in this ancient ritual. I have no illusions, either, but I have cast my lot with this great cat and will see the story through to its conclusion. Perhaps I will serve as an offering to his desired mate, and tonight I will be eaten. Oddly, I am not afraid; merely thoughtful and curious.

The sun sinks into the shimmering horizon as my lord follows the scent for hour upon hour. He would fain have left me in the dust, but I am fleet of foot if need be, and I follow at a safe distance. The sky is a bruise, puffy with swollen clouds that suck down the last rays of the sun, when my lord king at last finds his quarry.

Before us, underneath the gnarled branches of an olive tree, lies a young lioness, made before all days to be a queen, tended by her puppyish sisters. Her coat glows with sunshine stolen from the day as she tussles playfully with her littermates.

My king does not ply her with words or wiles, but courts her tenderly, nipping at her throat-fur and pawing at her tail as she turns away. He groans and growls, but I do not hear anything resembling a purr.

Suddenly, a sound of fury and jealousy rips from the grasses, and an older lion pounces on my lord. It seems that this queen of cats has already been claimed.

He is mature, this rival; he is not grey-furred yet, but he has the benefit of more summers than my lord has. His wits are as sharp as his teeth, and the battle that rages between the two is so fierce and flashing that it dwarfs even the thunderstorm that breaks out of the sky and begins to pound the grass.

Thunder concusses the air around us, and when the next strike of lightning rips through the evening air, it grounds itself in the olive tree, splitting it in two and igniting the splinters with skyfire. The fire snaps and growls, and the big cats snarl and roll, oblivious to the danger that surrounds them. Prudence chases the lady lioness and her attendants into the grass, in the direction of some shelter where I do not anticipate welcome. Instead, I press my back against a large boulder, its surface exhaling the heat of the day with the steam of sublimated raindrops, and I cover my head with my hands in a futile instinct of self-protection. The sucking roar of the fire and the rattling drums in the sky each compete for my attention, but I cannot look away from the lions at their battle. I feel the doom of blood and death in my simian bones.

My lord king and the master of the pride are well matched. What my king lacks in experience, he makes up for with his freshness, his enthusiasm a foil against the older lion's apparent cynicism. Their moves are a dance of slashing limbs and twisting torsos, and more often than not claws rake through fur instead of piercing hide, for each lion is swift in his response to the other's attacks. First blood is long in coming, and when it appears, the driving rain washes it so quickly from the wound that it is impossible to tell who bleeds. Scarlet swirls eddy in the runoff that seeks a sink in the parched land, the only evidence of the brutality of the conflict. Lightning traces wicked fingers in the purple sky, illuminating feline faces contorted with rage.

It ends as suddenly as the downpour does. The burnt tree sizzles quietly in the background as the older lion rolls onto his back, briefly showing throat. That it is surrender is plain for all to see, but when my lord goes in for the kill, the older lion rolls again quickly and dashes away. It is not a day of death after all.

My heart does not slow its pounding for hours.

The next morning, my lord king resumes his courtship of the sunlit lioness and her sisters. Shaped as I am by human story, I wish I could tell a tale of beauty and romance, but after all, even a noble lion is truly nothing more than a beast. That is most apparent when it comes to instinct's demands on existence. We eat as animals, we sleep as animals; we return our wastes to the earth, and we obey the calls of the wheel of life. It is not unworthy, to fulfill one's nature in this way, and the cubs born of these pairings will be truly magnificent cats, should they live.

Male lions are not domestic, and quickly become restless with frustrated wanderlust. After a full hand of rain-washed days with his new pride, my lord desires to retrace his progress and mark the entire range of his territory with the musk scent of possession and the sounds of his new words. If the lionesses do not rejoice to see us leave, neither are they sorry; our speech is a mystery to them, and they prefer a return to what is natural. One healthy male is as good as another, and the company of sisters is preferred to that of mates.

The small cats have paid their tribute, and they will return to their solitary hunting habits.

The grazers will no longer skirt near us to catch sight of the savior, but will scatter at his slightest scent. The time of redemption from the maneater has passed, and my lord king has become what he is: the reigning lion of a large land and fertile pride measuring his wealth. This time we walk alone, my lord the lion and his servant, a particular hamadryas.

THREE

Lion

THE SOFT SHADOWS of twilight rouse me from my nap, and I rise to continue the grand survey of my land, the task that stretches behind me and before me, enticing with its rhythms and varieties. It pleases me to receive tribute from my subjects, and I trot expectantly towards the scent of a nearby herd, anticipating that a roe deer will offer herself for my evening repast. The herds render of themselves, culling their sick and weak for the benefit of my protection. They know that men will not pursue them long into the lands where a lion reigns.

The herd has traveled briskly, and I follow their spoor throughout the night, loping along to the trill of insects and the trickle of runoff from the week's rains. As dawn breaks, I find the roe deer, but something is amiss. They pant in terror, circling around their fawns and stamping their hooves on the earth. The acrid smell of fear clouds like a miasma around their trembling bodies, and I restrain the urge to give chase. The herd has already been hunted.

There is a sense of wrongness that seeps from men, smirching the ground where they walk. It is like the sour smell of their sweat, the reek perceived not with my nose, but by something behind my eyes. This wrongness stains the field beneath the blood-splashed grass and the remains of my roe deer. Men have been here, robbing me. If they thought to do me tribute with this offal left behind, they have misjudged my character and do not fear me as they should.

I tread lightly around the scene of slaughter, nosing the matted grasses and pawing at the messy remains of the human hunt. Involuntarily my maw distends with a roar of pain—a discarded shard of metal has pierced my front paw like a thorn. It offends me and it wounds me.

There is a sound immediately behind me; I assume it is that baboon that refuses to leave me be, she who vexes me with words I do not always understand, and I do not immediately turn to acknowledge her. It is not fitting for a mere primate to witness my regal person yowling like a scorpion-stung cub. It comes as a great surprise, then, when a man comes into the corner of my vision. Because he does not stink like his comrades, I have not sensed his humanity near me. Even more startling is that this man does not rabbit away like the others always do.

He stands in the east, and the red sun outlines the figure of a man clothed in rags.

"Hush, hush. Hush, hush," he murmurs. I, who respect no one, am irrationally obedient to the sounds of his mouth.

Slowly he walks towards me, judging my temper before taking each step. It is clear that he seeks not to frighten me, and I do not wish to humiliate myself before him by showing any sign of distress. He kneels before my flank, hand outstretched.

"Well, then, your highness. I will help, if you'll allow me. But you must lie down, for if you move too quickly you threaten to trample me." His voice is warm, and a chuckle runs through it like a runnel of living water.

Though I marvel at the movement, I settle on my haunches and offer him my foreleg. A sense of calm has stolen over me, and I wish only to see what this man before me will do next.

"Hush, hush. Here we go." He pushes my shoulder towards the ground, and I roll onto my side, not quite showing throat, but close enough. I briefly hope that there is no creature around to see me. Then the man's hands wrap around my paw, radiating a warmth that penetrates deeper than the sunshine that worships me. I suppress a whine as he sits down, his back against a rock, and grasps the metal piece with one hand.

He braces his feet against my chest and wrenches the shard out.

Anticipating great pain, I open my mouth to roar, and the man swats me on the nose as if I am a cub. Too surprised for offense, my teeth clack shut.

Perhaps more surprising is that I do not retaliate, nor do I feel any instinct or desire to do so.

"Silly kitty." He smooths the fur of my mane, stroking with the grain, then lifts my injured paw onto his lap. He gentles me for a moment, rubbing the muscles in my foreleg, then tears a strip of cloth from his ragged garments. Very quickly, he brushes the grains of sand and bits of dirt away from the wound, rinses it with water from his drinking flask, then wraps my paw with the cloth. As the pain fades with the pressure of the linen, I suddenly become aware that this man does not pollute the earth at all. There is no stench, no sense of wrongness. Being next to him is akin to drinking from a cold mountain spring shaded by thick, breathing trees.

He refines the ground around him, making the air crisp and clear the way it is after the sun burns the fog out of the valley.

All of these things I feel in my bones, and this man simply moves around me, doing those things humans must do to care for themselves. He builds a fire, retrieves water from the nearby hole where the herd of roe refresh themselves, and boils it in a pot from his traveling sack. He sings the whole time, quiet songs with words whose meanings just escape my comprehension, but which sound like rest and repose.

He squats to eat, and after a while he trains his attention towards me.

"You are watching me, aren't you, your

highness?" He smiles, as if I am amusing to him. Imagine! A lion, amusing. I am mildly offended, and roll a soft growl around in my throat. He immediately understands me, much to my astonishment.

"No, cat, don't be offended, for I don't think you're silly. Quite the opposite. You are teaching me now, you see. The mysteries of your presence have answered questions I did not even know I should ask, though I have searched for many years. The mercies of the Lord are new from day to day, even in pondering the lion who sits before me, thinking his leonine thoughts."

His tone of voice appeals to my pride, and I sneeze in response to the pleasure of his attention, which feels like the tickle of dust in the afternoon sunlight. It is right that lions should inspire such awe, for a lion is walking majesty; and it is meet that lions should inspire fear as well, for we are fearsomely powerful. I begin to groom my glorious coat, knowing that he is watching and basking in the warmth of his gaze.

"Would you like to know what I see, puss?" Again, his voice is colored with a smile, and I pause, mid-ablution.

"You are a beautiful cat, young and strong. The Lord has woven the light of the stars into your soft and shining coat, and your eyes are bright like polished jasper. You have been wounded recently, but your wounds heal cleanly, so I see that you are healthy and well-fed. You are also very proud, and some of that is deservedly so, for you are a delightful creature. But some of that is false pride, for you have not made yourself to be as you are, you know. You are the lion you were made to be, not any more and not any less. And as lovely as you are, you still smell like a cat." He wrinkles his nose and laughs.

My tail twitches as he gazes into my eyes, and it is then that I remember the words shared with that particular hamadryas, Astennu, words that have pestered me all of these moons. *Why should you be particular? Isn't it enough to be hamadryas?*

Perhaps, lord, it would be enough if I had never known it differently.

In this moment, I begin to feel it. I am not just lion in the presence of this man. I am a particular lion, and he sees me—he sees me as something more than I thought I was. This is a thing that, once beheld, cannot be unseen. Everything I know must change. The skin at the base of my tail begins to tingle in the presence of this revelation, in acknowledgment of his authority over me. Lion I may be—lord of the savanna and brush and all creatures great and small—but I am not the king of this man, and that is very good.

Deep within, I feel a rumble begin, a warm and rolling sound like thunder dying in the distance. I exhale an unfamiliar vibration that lingers in my throat and travels past the gates of my teeth, tickling my whiskers and buzzing the air around my muzzle like heat rising from the hot sand. In the presence of this astonishing man, I learn the first surprise of a lion's purr: that it begins with submission. I wonder if my lioness mother knew this much.

It is a truth as unshakeable as the rock on which I lie. I am no longer my own master—I will follow this man until the end of my days.

Baboon

 CAN SEE EVERYTHING from my hiding place behind an ash-covered boulder. This man has worked some sorcery on my lord king, has woven a spell more powerful than any I have heard uttered in dark, chthonic voices by the men who reared me in the shadows of the shrines. His magic is powerful and fearsome, and I watch in awe as he fondles the mane of the lordly lion with the confidence of a maiden with a temple cat asleep on her lap. All afternoon he cares for the lion's sore paw with tenderness and solicitude.

I cannot hear his words, but all through-out the heat of the day, he alternately sings or speaks, sharing with the lion the water from his flask and the food from his pot. It is curious and unnerving to watch a king lap lentils from a dish like a kitten laps cream from a saucer.

As the sun arcs across the sky, I creep through the grass to be closer to this miracle. Finally, I am close enough to hear what passes between them.

The lion has rolled onto his back, mewling quietly at the man.

I offer you fealty. You own my life.

"You offer me a great gift, puss, but I can-not accept such a regal sacrifice. You are a king, made to rule the savanna. I imagine you have a whole pride of lady-queens who await your return from wandering—cubs to swat and roe deer to chase."

The lion rolls onto his belly and looks intently at the man, pleading with his large yellow eyes. I have never seen such an expression on the face of a lion before.

That is nothing compared to what you have already given me. I am yours forever, man.

"Sweet lion, I am honored beyond imagining. I send you forth to your life with my blessing. You are free."

The lion belly-crawls to the cross-legged man and lays his head in his lap. A moment later, his large and raspy tongue begins to lave the man's feet. The man erupts in laughter and wriggles his legs, then reaches forward and throws his arms around the shaggy mane.

If not a slave, will you take a friend?

Still laughing, his face buried in the lion's soft fur, the man says, "Yes, your highness. I will have you as a friend, for as long as you desire."

I cannot bear the mystery any longer. I creep out from the grasses and into the clearing.

The man looks up in surprise, glancing quickly between the lion and me, measuring the potential for danger. The lion himself will not look at me at all. The man's face lights up.

"Ah, I see. You two know each other."

How he perceives this, when the lion is trying with all of his might to pretend that I do not exist, I do not know. I bound lightly to the man and I am struck instantly by the pleasure of his company. He smells of temple incense and the scent of water.

Reared by men, I have learned mostly to avoid them, to approach for handouts only when their faces are soft, and to fear them when necessary, which is often enough. Occasionally, though, I have learned to care for them. The priest who hand-fed me as a baby I came closest to loving; he was kind, held me gently in his arms when the racket of thunderstorms frightened me, and taught me the myths of the temple. When I grew to full size, he would sometimes allow me to pick the lice from his hair, though he rarely returned the affection with more than a gentle pat on the head. There was also a kitchen girl who fed me fruit scraps and sang me the songs of her village. If I had never met this man now standing before me, I would have thought those two the best humanity had to offer.

This man is something else altogether.

I trot over to face my lord.

Will you eat me? My movement asks him, for as changed as he is, I am afraid to speak to him.

He whines in a most undignified manner. *No.* What is this bizarre development?

"I would stay with him, if I were you," I offer in words, tentative and unsure of how to be with such a lion.

"I am lion. This is all very unusual," he complains, embarrassed.

"Not more unusual than he is." I gesture at the miracle man with an open palm.

"I fear that becoming a particular lion will make me less of a lion, but I cannot turn away. If I return to reign as king, I will always wonder what could have been and I will never be content. This man has stolen my satisfaction, and I am grateful to him for it."

I hear the agony in the lion's voice, and I find that I care for him more as this new, unsure creature than I did when he was merely my arrogant lord king. I hold out my hand towards him.

"Let us test this tension together," I say. "There is only one way through this now, I think."

The man watches us intently while we speak with each other, glancing back and forth as if he understands what we are saying, though that is impossible. He makes no sound or song.

"What of you, Astennu?" the lion asks.

"I shall follow whatever you choose, lord lion. If you return to the savanna, I will follow you and eventually find a band of baboons to join. Though I admit I am curious about this man, and if you go with him, I will be two steps behind you."

He watches his paw as it stirs the dust.

"If I don't follow him now, I'll never know what particular kind of lion I could be."

"It is worthy, lion. I think we will not regret it."

He looks up at my face, and I wonder again whether I have crossed over the line from companion to dinner.

The man clears his throat.

"I must return to my home now, puss, your highness. You and the baboon may follow as long as you wish, and turn back whenever you desire."

He runs his hand over the lion's russet mane, then holds it out to me. With trepidation born of experience, I extend the whole length of my arm and touch his fingertips. It is like when the lightning struck the olive tree, only the fire that ignites me crackles merrily in my heart. His mouth breaks into a beaming smile, and I feel the muscles in my face mirroring him in response, my teeth bared in a silliness that is not threat. Even when I lived in the temple, I mimicked human smiles rarely, feeling them unnatural. He laughs in delight.

The man turns to leave in the cool of the twilight. The lion pads beside him, and I trail behind the pair, deep in thought. Who has ever heard of a lion as a slave, let alone a devoted friend?

We journey through the night and late into the next morning, beyond the arid edges of our known territory. We stop to rest for the afternoon in a patch of palm and olive trees that breaks up the endlessness of the scrubby desert.

He points to the northwest. "That way lies the great sea, my friends. Can you smell the salt in the air?" He stares off in the distance, inhales a lungful of air, and gestures across his body with his right hand.

The lion and I exchange a glance, and though we do not know what we are searching for, we lift our snouts to the wind and breathe deeply. Faintly, far off in the distance, the air blows with an unfamiliar tang that promises some eventual adventure. To think of the future is strange for beasts, and in a moment, the lion and I both shake our heads to clear them. After our rest in the oasis, we continue on our strange pilgrimage.

The man is quiet most of the time, which is much different from what I expected. Every so often, he pauses and looks to the sky, as if he is having a conversation with the clouds and must listen so that they can answer him. We spend the nights in any oasis we can find, and many mornings later our journey brings us to the bank of a great river. Grasses and reeds cluster at the edges of the muddy brown water, which smells earthy and baked.

He pauses at the bank, then removes his sandals.

"Baboon and lion, we approach the realm of men. Do you still wish to carry on with me, or have you chosen to return to your wilderness and wildness?"

Neither of us looks back, nor do our faces turn in the slightest. The man approaches the lion.

"Are you sure you will stay, your highness?"

The lion whuffs gently in reply.

"And you, madam hamadryas?"

I nod in response, a mannerism I remember from my temple days.

"Then I think it must be this way. It will be very unusual, but if you will not return to the typical lives of beasts, you must be set apart somehow. If you will stay by my side, you must first descend into the Jordan."

I cock my head at the man, wondering if he means to bathe us. Temple-reared, it would not be my first experience of that particular indignity, but I wonder how the cat will handle it.

The man wades out into the water and begins to sing again, strange words, low and sweet. He calls to the heavens and holds his arms out to his sides, his face tipped to the sky. A shaft of sunlight pierces the clouds and sparkles on the rolling current. Then he beckons to the lion.

The lion wades awkwardly into the river, which comes up to his chin. He has little natural

grace in the water, though he can swim compe-
tently enough if he needs to. The man places his
hand on the top of the lion's head, calls out in
a loud voice, and presses the lion's head firmly
below the surface.

I stifle a yelp. Does the man think to drown
the lion? Does he not know how strong the big
cat truly is?

The lion roars as his head breaks the surface
of the water, and my heart pounds in anticipation of the coming violence. Surely the lion will
punish the man for his attempted murder. But
the roar I hear is one of joy, and the man cups
the leonine face in his hands and kisses his eyes.

"I christen you Jordanes, in the name of the
Father, and of the Son, and of the Holy Spirit.
Amen."

The lion paddles back out of the water with a
silly, doglike grin on his face.

"Have you heard, hamadryas? I now have a
name."

I am speechless.

The man holds out his hand to me. For a moment, I consider turning back, seeking out the savanna, and discovering a troop of baboons in need of a young female. My arms can almost feel the weight of an infant at my breast, its fingers tangled in my fur, and I long for that moment with all of the weight in my soul.

And yet . . .

I do not know what questions I have to ask, but I know in my heart that this man holds the answers. I must follow this path first, before I turn aside and rest in my hamadryas nature. I wonder what he will name me.

I swim gracefully out to the man and lean back onto his arm, closing my eyes in fear and anticipation of the strange ablution. He sings again, a song of planted peace and embraced death and new life springing forth, and my trembling stills. Then my head descends beneath the waters.

My ears are suddenly full of the white-blue sound of rushing water, and the muffled pulse of the man's words elongates to fit this strange, timeless moment. There is an instant, as a creature dies, where the veil is very thin and easily parted. I have seen a hyena there, in that liminal present, perk up his ears and cock his head, as if hearing the summons of a beloved voice. I have seen a gazelle lay herself down willingly, baring her neck proudly and gently as the light left her eyes.

Under the water, I feel the eye of my heart open, and I see what they saw, beholding the great mystery. There are no words for the wonder, and the blood in my veins leaps with joy.

I rise with a gasp.

"I christen you Astennu, in the name of the Father, and of the Son, and of the Holy Spirit. Amen."

Astennu.

My name.

He knows my name.

Fullness washes over me like the rainshower in the desert, and I weep.

The man carries me onto the shore and lays me gently beside Jordanes, the lordly lion.

"Well now, my precious ones. Now that you have your names, you must also learn mine. For I am not just human, but a particular one. You may call me Gerasim."

FIVE

Jordanes

E CROSS THE river at a natural ford, my paws plashing in the shallow water, and begin to climb a steep path. Before us rises a white-walled hive of men built into the side of the cliff, and the stony windows teem with hidden motion. The men in the common places are like termites, busy and buzzing, but every one of them falls silent as we walk past, my master Gerasim, the baboon, and I. We approach a center square, and even more men descend from caves carved in the sheer stone to come meet us. Whether they are rank or repellent, I cannot say, for my master covers it all with a mineral scent.

A hysterical voice breaks the silence.

"You can't possibly mean to keep him, Abbot!"

There is a swell of disapproval in the crowd, like the murmur of wind in the grass. Gerasim smiles to himself and scans the crowd for the speaker.

A fleshy man waddles forward, hands on his hips.

"Really, Abbot. This is going too far. This is a monastery, not a circus!"

Gerasim holds his hands out in front of himself and shrugs. "I did not bring them here, Abba Joseph. These creatures have followed me of their own accord, wishing to learn something of the ways of the Lord."

Abba Joseph scoffs. "The violence of nature and instinct are the only ways they will ever know. They are beasts, Abba Gerasim, and they belong in the wilds."

Gerasim bows his head and is silent for a moment. When he speaks, it is so quiet that all of the brothers lean forward to hear him, bending like grass in the wind.

"I, too, was a beast once. And the Lord led me here, and here it was that he made me a real man."

Another, younger voice pipes up.

"Abba Gerasim, we have no meat—he will devour us while we sleep!"

Gerasim smiles at this. "Oh, no, Abba Macarius. Jordanes is no maneater, that I can assure you. He finds the whole notion abhorrent."

"Fool!" cries a third voice. "It is a wild beast, you cannot know what it will or will not do. At the very least he will eat the donkey!"

My master does not respond with words this time, but holds his hand up for silence. He turns and deliberately grasps my face in his strong hands, and kneels with his forehead pressed against my teeth. I whuff gently and lick his cheek. Then he grasps my ears in his fists and twists my head onto the ground. He places his foot upon my face.

"Jordanes will not hurt you. Be not afraid."

Even so, the monks before us tremble.

"What of the baboon?" calls a voice from the back of the crowd. "My cousin had a pet one that bit off his finger when it outgrew its baby-hood. They, too, are violent and unpredictable."

Gerasim nods and lays a finger beside his nose.

"Astennu, my love, come here."

The shy hamadryas lopes over to him and takes his outstretched hand with the confidence of a human child.

"You were not raised in the wild, were you, my dear?"

She shakes her head no, and the crowd gasps.

"My guess is that you are a holy beast from the back country, where the old gods reign in shrinking pockets. Are you of Thoth's temple?"

Her eyes are bright with wonder as she nods in affirmation.

"A circus trick! It is nothing more than a

circus trick!" screeches a new voice, and the murmuring of the crowd surges into a gravelly grumble. My muscles tense in response to the change in tone.

Gerasim cups the baboon's face in his right hand and gently strokes her ears with his left. Then he turns his stern gaze upon the brothers, and the volume of the group quickly subsides. I am reminded of how Gerasim swatted my nose before I could roar at him, back before I was Jordanes, what seems like ages ago.

"Brothers, you have nothing to fear from her. The hermetic spirit has infected her with the desire for wisdom, and now she must chase it down whatever path lies before her. She wishes only to remain with Jordanes and me at the moment. Isn't that so, love?"

Astennu reaches out tentatively and pets Gerasim's beard, picking gently at imaginary lice. I cannot help but sneeze in amusement—surely the hamadryas will never try something so informal with me, her liege.

The crowd before us murmurs, then begins to disperse. Gerasim has had the last word.

We are approached by a youth with no hair on his face, who holds his hands out in a cup and kneels before Gerasim.

Gerasim makes a motion in the air, and the youth kisses his hand.

"What can I do for you, young Gregory?"

"Abba Gerasim, may I touch them?"

"You'll have to ask them," he chuckles.

"But they are beasts! They won't understand me. Surely they only listen to their trainer!" Gregory protests.

"Give it a try, young Gregory. These are not just any lion and baboon, they are Jordanes and Astennu, and they are not trained beasts. They are unique among their kinds, and the Lord has set them before us as treasures of His wisdom. I do not know what we will learn from them, but nevertheless, they are here for a reason."

The youth kneels and reaches towards me.

"Jordanes, may I touch you?" he asks

breathlessly. His reverence pleases me.

In response, I press my nose against his hand. The youth shudders in a spasm of fear and delight, then sighs deeply. He runs his fingers through my mane, gently picking at the tangles.

"Abba Gerasim, I shall like this very much," he says. Gerasim only smiles.

And so begins our life at the monastery.

જ્જ

WHEN I WAKE in the morning I am given bread and dates with my master and his monks, and to my surprise, they are finer than the plumpest roe deer ever offered readily. Astennu watches me with amusement in her simian eyes, daintily ripping a date into small pieces before placing them in her mouth. I, however, can fit three or more dates in the roll of my tongue, and I do so with relish.

In the lavra, everyone has his labor, and I am charged with guarding the donkey that grazes on the bank of the river. He is a stupid creature,

※ 63 ※

and every noise he makes is one of complaint. He has the simple task of carrying water from the river back to the monastery to supplement the cisterns. I do not comprehend why he would not gladly serve my master and his monks, but he is idle and stubborn through and through. His laziness smells like the manure that dries on his hooves.

"He is not like us at all," I explain to Astennu, on one of the donkey's return trips to the monastery. The hamadryas has spent the day in the shadow of our master.

She nods. "The only thing his body says is 'no'. Does he hear you when you speak?"

"He hears only the growl of a lion, and fears me."

"That is not good, my lord."

"I know."

When the donkey is brought in for the day, I pad gratefully behind my master to his cell, a rounded room whittled out of the bones of the chalky cliff. I lie against his feet as he kneels on the stone floor, murmuring and singing words like dark honey. Even though the ground is hard, the cool exhalation of the rock walls is refreshing after the hot day in the sun. Contentment fills my bones, rising from the tip of my tail to fill my throat. Joy spills out in sound, and my lion-purr becomes an ison for the melody of Gerasim's prayer.

All is peace in our little cell, and we sleep the sleep of safety.

But in the morning, the monks are still afraid of me.

ॐ

THE DAYS ARE much the same. I breakfast with the skittish monks, guard the stupid donkey, and bask in the presence of my master. Young Gregory pats my head when he passes me in the plaza of the lavra, but he is not yet a monk like the others and scurries about here and there in his enthusiasm to prove himself. He has little time to spend on me, which is acceptable. I do not need the attentions of these strange men. It is enough that I cannot sense any foulness about them, and I find their nervousness amusing.

One night, after all of the monks have retired to their cells, Gerasim does not kneel to pray. Instead, he puts his finger beside his nose and smiles.

"Come, my friends. I have something to show you. But we must go now, so that the other monks will not be frightened."

Astennu and I share a glance, and fall in step immediately behind our master. He leads us down a network of stone hallways, lower down and deeper into the cliff itself. Finally, we come to a room that is barred by a gold and purple curtain. Gerasim parts the veil to reveal a small chapel, the walls covered with painted images. He points to one on the far side, an image of a human baby wrapped in cloth, surrounded by beasts. Astennu and I share a look of surprise, and the baboon scampers up to the painting, gesturing at the animals.

"Yes, my dear. Our Lord has always included the animals in his stories. Here it shows that on the night of his birth, an ox and an ass kept vigil. So, you see, you and his highness have joined a long tradition of beasts that have consecrated themselves to the Lord."

I rumble in assent, though I note with some disappointment that no lion has been depicted.

"When the holy family fled from evil men, they stayed here, in this very room. An old man, a young woman, a baby, and a donkey."

I whuff in disbelief. *Donkeys are stupid and lazy.*

"Not all donkeys are as obstinate as our monastery's beast. The Lord must favor them, Jordanes, for they play many roles in his stories."

I yawn, not impressed.

"Well, then. I see that you are not convinced. Perhaps our donkey is only donkey right now, and has not yet chosen to become a particular donkey. It is a difficult decision, your majesty, as you well know. Perhaps he is not even called to it, or is not capable of it. Now, let us pray."

The man, the baboon, and I, the lion, kneel down before the image of the holy ox and ass and the human baby whom they worship, and together we make the music of our prayers in the chapel in the heart of the hill.

❧

TODAY MUST BE a feast, for Abba Poemen feeds me a breakfast of lentils in addition to the dates that I continue to find delightful. He grins nervously when I lick his hand but strokes my mane in return. I think he will warm to me in time.

The sun is scorching already as I lead the donkey, that churlish brute, to his shrinking patch of green. Already he is braying his complaint, and I indulge in a fantasy of silencing his loud asininity with a quick crunch of bones.

Remorse for the rudeness of my reflection claws me quickly; blood thoughts have been far from my mind since living in the lavra. Such violence perishes in the presence of my master.

I muffle a growl at the donkey and sprawl in a cool patch of rushes to watch him eat. Sleep steals softly over my eyes.

Astennu shakes me awake hours later.

"Jordanes, rouse yourself."

I yawn and growl, ready to roll over and resume my nap.

"Jordanes, you have been gone too long. I came looking for you. Where is the donkey?"

Where is the donkey?

I sit up and look towards the river. The stupid creature is gone.

I bite back a roar, and Astennu leaps back into the rushes in her fright. Particular or not, the hamadryas still does not trust me not to eat her in my anger. She is much like the monks in her fear. I leap to my feet and charge into the rushes. Astennu's voice, calling my name, fades in the distance.

I roam through the day and the rest of the night, searching for scent on both sides of the river, but the donkey has completely disappeared. All that remains is the wind on the sand that is tainted by men most decidedly not the monks I have grown fond of. The ground itself carries the stink of sewage and carrion, and I know them to be evil men by the tarry miasma that lingers.

Reluctantly, I return to the lavra.

My master Gerasim meets me at the gate.

"Oh, Jordanes. Astennu has told me of your misfortune."

Just then, fat Abba Joseph, the monastery steward, waddles into the courtyard.

"Where is the donkey? Abba Gerasim, the beast has devoured the donkey!" he cries in a loud voice.

Monks within earshot leave their tasks and gather in the plaza.

"I knew it was a mistake to let the creature live with us," says Abba Macarius.

"Are you sure it was Jordanes?" asks Abba Poemen timidly.

"What else could it have been?" Abba

Macarius snaps. "Who will carry our water now? Just look what this foolishness has cost us. You cannot tame a wild animal."

"Jordanes isn't wild," young Gregory pipes up.

"Quiet, boy! Or you'll be hauling water eight miles a day."

"What shall we do now?" asks Abba Joseph, wringing his hands.

I drag my mane on the ground in sorrow.

My master stands behind my shoulders, and I savor the coolness of his peace as it passes over me. He places his bright hand upon my head, and a rill of glad laughter ripples his voice.

"Do not be angry at Jordanes. Don't you see? He is a very sorry lion. Jordanes, will you carry the water, now that our donkey is no longer with us?"

In response, I pad lightly to the earthenware jars, nosing them gently. The monks are speechless in their surprise, all except Gregory, who crows in delight.

"I told you he wasn't wild! Look at him. He understands everything."

But of all the monks, only young Gregory can look at me without fear. I see suspicion in their eyes, the belief that after all, I am only lion. It saddens me more than I expect, for I find that I have desired to become a particular lion— Jordanes, a lion of peace and service—to all of them, and not only my master. I resolve to win their trust.

And so begins my repentance.

Astennu

HE SUN CHASES the moon; she whirls in and out of hiding again and again, marking the time of our indenture.

The brothers no longer pretend to tolerate my lord lion, but avoid him utterly or revile him to his face. It is a marker of the change in him that Jordanes bears this with nary a growl or whine. They do not care for me, either, but I give them little cause for concern, for I rarely leave Gerasim's side.

Even Abba Poemen fears to care for the lion

now, and our Gerasim goes himself into the storeroom each morning to retrieve the bread and dates for our breakfasts. Often there is no food set aside at all for the lion, as if the monks desire that Jordanes fail this test of hunger and prove his mere bestiality. I have seen the poor, pathetic cat attempt to fill his belly with riparian grasses, and the sight twists my mouth with pity. He grows thin, but persists in his repentance. I wonder what he is trying to prove, and to whom: is it the brothers' prejudices he strives against, or his own? What is the point of all this suffering?

Gerasim tightens the straps of the water harness around Jordanes's body, singing his prayers as he cinches the buckle. He pats the big cat's rump gently, sending him on his way to fill the water jars. I watch as the lowly lion carefully makes the steep descent from the cliffs, loping over the dry meadows and around the acacia trees, completing the journey of about four miles as swiftly as he is able. He makes so many trips each day that sometimes I lose count—though I can count the ripple of ribs on his side.

Occasionally I travel with him, keeping him company as he goes down to the river.

"Do you really think they will forgive you, Jordanes? They think you a killer."

"They will if they follow our master. They will see."

"What if they don't?"

"They will." He pauses, then adds, "You no longer fear me."

I think on this. It is true. Somehow, since the loss of the donkey, I have lost my suspicion of being a snack saved for later. Perhaps it is the persistence with which he chews the stringy grass.

"Something has changed between us. I do not understand it, but I do not doubt it. You will not eat me."

He nods his great head. "I will never eat you. Since the night in the chapel, and especially since the donkey."

Jordanes wades into the water, paddling about gently as the river rushes to fill the jars. I wait for him at the top of a *doum* tree, picking handfuls of ripe dates to pass the time. He trudges out, burdened with the heavy water jars, and I scamper down the tree with an offering.

He eats them too quickly, and his shrinking stomach protests. He makes a hacking, gagging sound, and I throw up my hands in exasperation.

"Jordanes, why do you not hunt here? Surely there is small game in the grasses, better food for a lion than dates and lentils. Here, let me fetch you a locust or two. You were not made to live this way." A note of pleading has crept into my voice, for my concern for my lord grows as his muscular flank diminishes.

"Astennu, I have not truly hungered for flesh since the day our master removed the metal thorn from my paw."

He turns away from me, walking slowly up the path to the monastery. His burdens, such as they are, are cumbersome, and I wonder if they are even bearable.

After lunch, Gerasim releases the lion from his duty.

"Dear puss, I would like you to rest this day. It is a blessed feast, the Exaltation of the Precious and Life-giving Cross, and the cisterns are full from yesterday's early storm. We do not need the extra water."

Jordanes sighs. He yearns to be welcomed back into the society of the brothers, but today is not the day. He looks at me, unwilling to ask for company, but the loneliness in his eyes breaks my heart. Gerasim gestures to me with a small wave.

I would rather join Gerasim in the sanctuary, for I love to hang from the top of a column support and bathe in the music of the monks' prayers, but I know where I am needed.

"I will accompany you again, your majesty."

This time, when I walk beside him, I rest my hand on his back, and when we stop to rest in the shade of a twisted olive tree, he lowers his great head and allows me to pick the tangles from his mane. The noise he makes is not quite a lion-purr, but a soothing thrum that lulls us both to the edge of sleep. I lean against his neck, burrowing against his warm side.

Suddenly, the lion's nose twitches, and he stands at attention. I tumble from my soft nest onto the rocky ground.

"Do you smell that, hamadryas?"

I shake my sleepy head in surprise, sneezing to clear the fog from my nose.

"I have not your olfactory skills, my lord," I admit after a moment.

"I smell laziness and dry manure."

I blink in confusion.

He stamps his paw impatiently. "Laziness and manure! The smell of the donkey."

"My lord, that could be any donkey within a hundred miles or more!"

"Sewage! And carrion!"

I step in front of him and grasp his furry face

in my hands.

"I cannot make sense of your words, Jordanes."

"It is the smell of evil men."

"There are many of those in the world, lion. It is also the smell of fetid waste and offal. It could be many things other than what you suppose—an oryx corpse torn by hyenas and vultures; a rotting patch of river mud. It could be any small-minded nomad beating the life out of his obstinate donkey."

"It is our donkey, Astennu, I am sure of it."

I hold up my hands in dismay. "But where? Your nose is so powerful, it could be days away, if they are even standing still."

He gazes off towards the sun, creeping to its rest in the west.

"That way."

He begins to trot away, then turns back to me.

"Go to Gerasim. Tell him where I have gone."

"How am I supposed to do that?" I gape at the lion.

"Foolish hamadryas. Do you not know by now that he hears every word that passes between us? Speak to him the way you speak to me, and he will hear you."

"Wait!" I stammer. "At least let me come with you."

"Not this time, Astennu. Some journeys must be taken alone."

He begins to run.

"Jordanes!" I call. "Come back!"

"I will!" he roars, his voice carrying back on the wind. "With the donkey!"

Then he is gone.

⌀

EVEN THOUGH I know Jordanes is right about Gerasim the moment he speaks the truth aloud, I am still cowed by the idea of speaking directly to our master. I gather my courage as I travel home to the monastery.

He meets me at the gate.

"Where is our cat, my love?" he asks gently.

I look him square in the eye.

"He caught a scent. He has gone to find the donkey."

Gerasim cocks his head and turns to the west. "I see."

He looks skyward, his finger by his nose, listening to some secret voice I cannot hear.

"It seems it will be a long journey for him. I wonder which of us will make it home first."

"Are we not home, master?" I ask, still wondering if it is truly possible that he will hear my question.

"We are going on a journey too, Astennu. It is a long one, and will take many weeks, and if you so desire, you will see the sea, my dear."

I flutter my lips in incomprehension.

"There is to be a great meeting in a faraway city called Chalcedon, and I must go. You may come with me if you wish, though you are free as always to return to the savanna if your time with us has ended."

"I will come," I say, reaching for my master's

hand as I reach out to him with words. "As much as it calls me, I still fear the wilderness. Without Jordanes, I am only a solitary hamadryas; and without you, there is no one who remembers my name."

Gerasim strokes my head.

"There is One who never forgets it, Astennu. Do not be afraid of your life, for you are never truly alone. Come now, and let us pray before our rest. We leave in the morning."

"But what of Jordanes, master? If he returns to the monastery before we do, I fear he will not be welcome."

"Our paths will cross again when the time is ripe for it. The machinations of destiny are in better hands than mine. But I think he will not return before we do, Astennu. Do not let your heart be troubled."

"But how do you know, Gerasim?" I plead, afraid for my friend.

Gerasim lets out a long sigh and seems to wrestle with a thought. He begins to speak, then stops. Finally he finds what he was searching for. "There is a third eye, Astennu, that we seek a kind of vision with. It is called the eye of the heart. It is one of many of the mysteries of being that I could teach you, the true Ways of the world that have not been corrupted by the evil in the hearts of men. I do not know, though, whether these things will help you on your journey. With the questions that trouble your heart."

I shiver in fear. "Hamadryas are not made for mystery, Gerasim. But my namesake Astennu was steeped in such things. I do not know what I want."

Gerasim nods thoughtfully as he strokes the fur on the back of my neck. I wait for his response, but it is long in coming, and I am wretched with the misery of unknowing. Finally, he breaks the silence.

"All of creation is to be made new, Astennu. I think that if I tell you the true Way of things, it cannot hurt you. The exact nature of the future is unclear to me, but I see no danger for you on this path. Will you speak with me, then? Come, let us reason together."

His voice is calm and trustworthy, and my fear melts away.

And so begins my becoming.

SEVEN

King of Beasts

WHEN I TURN and race away from the hamadryas, my flesh is filled with the exhilaration of the hunt. Blood rushes through my reins, and the brightness of fresh air gulped in exertion enlightens my eyes. I am fully lion, in the Now—my awareness as Jordanes takes second place to the cascade of instinct and response. The scent I follow is faint, but I am certain of the direction. It is sheer joy to be nothing but lion again, at least for the moment.

This quest is a retracing of my steps, a review

of my life's journey, and my awareness of its meaning is certainly not that of a mere lion. Lions do not feel torn between two paths, nor do they feel any conflict within themselves from moment to moment. After a few days of solitary chase, I enter the range of my former pride, and my first challenge arises. I am afflicted with concern for my lioness and her sisters, for the scent I chase has passed through this place. Has my absence brought misfortune to these innocents? If so, it grieves my heart. I choose the detour and scout the range of my lady's lands.

I am ready to rest during the noon heat when my nose crinkles at the scent of a patch of grass dotted with dried lion blood. Tufts of downy lion hairs are matted to a shrub, and a man's arrowshaft lies broken on the sand. I growl, low and menacing, for violence has been done to my pride. But is it still mine? Perhaps I have no right to be here any longer. Rather than rest with the questions that haunt me, I continue on, hoping with my lionheart to find that the injury given was not severe.

I locate the pride late in the afternoon, lazing near a shallow watering hole—my sunlit lioness queen and her noble sisters, and at least two, maybe three, litters of growing cubs. As I count them I realize that the victim must be a missing lion cub, and again a growl rises in my throat. It is the natural order of things for predators to hunt the small and weak, the old and the young, but I find I am not at peace with the so-called natural order of things any longer.

The lioness watches me wrestle with my thoughts, her prudence determining whether or not I am a threat to her offspring and those of her sisters. I see no personal recognition in her eyes, no acknowledgment of ownership or particularity—but why should there be? She is lion, after all, and she reigns over her sinuous sisters and their bouncing cubs in their golden mornings. I watch the tiny creatures play, rolling and tumbling in the dust under the tree. I cannot be certain that they are all mine, for I did not linger long in their land and am too far away to smell them individually, but it matters not. I have left all thoughts of competition in that former life. I wonder if one of the little kittens would grow to stalk my own swishing tail through the savanna grass on the brink of his maturity. These are not lion thoughts, and I yawn to clear my head.

I do not approach the pride; I see now it is not mine to own. I have chosen a different way. I only dip my head in greeting to the royal lady, turn, and walk away. It is sufficient now to see that they live, and to know that vengeance will be mine.

I return to the scent, and my hunt brings me to the scorched olive tree, the place where the land bears the scars of what I had thought to be the greatest battle of my life. Had I remained only lion, it would have been simple and true. But now I am Jordanes the lion, and have found a deeper battle that drives me harder, and I will not relent until my dying breath.

Now I recall the steps of my royal progress,

the creatures who made note of my presence. The pageantry seems absurd to me now, and I wonder at the motives of those smaller felines that accompanied me. In my pride, I assumed obeisance; in my memory, I see that I provided them with some unknown advantage. Perhaps pride is little more than deception—a feeble attempt to hide the truth.

Later I pass under an ancient acacia, perhaps the very one where Astennu first began to speak with words above our first primitive exchanges. I recall her question that infected me with the quest for particularity, and I answer her now: Yes, Astennu, if a lion can be less than lion, then I gamble with my life that he can also be more.

I AM RECLINING in the shade of an ancient oak tree, resting from the tired rays of the autumn sun, when the wind wafts a scent of laziness and dry manure in my direction, this time strong and pungent. I rise in instant attention. I quietly stalk through the grass, searching for the source. My lionheart thrums with purpose and anticipation; my nerves are steady and sure. I choose the exact moment of every footfall, and I am as silent as the sun as he slips behind a cloud.

I find my prey at a watering hole, the donkey tethered loosely to a tree, accompanied by six sweaty men cocooned in filthy dark linens that wrap them like graveclothes. They sprawl like a fungus in their hastily erected tents, their wrongness seeping into the oasis around them, rotting the good earth beneath it. A tiny lion skin is stretched upon a rack in front of the campfire, and a man squats near, hunched over a stick which he works with his knife.

The birds that remain in the trees are silent in their witness; most have flown away. The only sounds that break the eerie hush are the muffled sob of a crying female and the scraping of the man's knife.

I choose every footfall.

These stupid men could not hear me even if

they tried, and their eyes are dimmed with drink.

Pouncing from the scrub, I roar as I have not roared in moons upon moons, since the day of the battle in the storm. The sound tears from my throat in a torrent of fury, and my leap carries me through the air like an avenging angel. In the heartbeat that I am airborne, their puffy faces stretch into the distorted shapes of fear—eyes round, mouths agape.

Then the stinking men scatter like rabbits. In my throttled rage, I give chase, bounding after first one ugly creature, then another, driving them over the dunes in different directions. It is a vicious joy to give them terrors that soil their robes, but I do not maim, nor do I kill. I chase them, I swat at them with my claws sheathed, I roar inches away from their faces, and I delight in every minute of the game. When their wills are broken and they lie half-dead in the defeated puddles of their cowardly fear, I return to the oasis to finish my task.

The donkey pants in fright at the sight of

me, square teeth bared and tongue swollen with stress. I glare at the stupid creature, then puff gently. I prostrate myself on the grass, laying my head on my paws, signaling no threat in every way I know how to. The donkey seems to respond, but when a stifled shriek alerts me that the human female remains hidden in her tent, the stupid creature rears in alarm.

I repeat my pantomime, aware that the eyes of every living thing are upon me—bird, beast, and human. Fear can only be sustained for so long without a cause, and gradually, the donkey's ears flop down in calm, and the female's breathing slows.

When the donkey is still, I arise and seize his rope in my mouth, gnawing at the terrible-tasting fibers. I swallow a growl of frustration, unwilling to frighten the donkey and repeat the entire process yet again.

"May—may I help?" a musical voice asks. She is timid, but the coppery smell of her fear is fading.

I step away from the tree while the woman

unties the knotted rope. Her hands work nimbly, but her eyes never leave me. I whuff gently in thanks, and she smiles in surprise.

"You are a very smart lion, aren't you?" she says, holding out the rope.

I yawn, then grab it with my mouth, tugging gently on the lead until the donkey begins to follow me meekly. He makes no complaint, though I urge him to walk quickly.

"Wait!"

I stop and rest my gaze on the woman, who retrieves a satchel from her tent and mounts the donkey.

"You are a clever lion and obviously have some task to complete. I know you understand me, so hear this: I will not impose on your hospitality, good lion. I only seek your protection, and to journey with you until we are away from the evil men."

I lick her hand with my raspy tongue and retrieve the donkey's lead.

The woman accompanies us for a day and a

night. She hums quietly while we walk, but does not speak again, though she is alert and watches me carefully. At the end of the second day, she gingerly brushes my mane with the back of her hand and takes her leave. She does not spare a look for the donkey as her form disappears in the distance, a black silhouette against the twilit desert sky.

The rest of the return is uneventful, if slower than I wish. The donkey is still stupid and obstinate, though he no longer fears me. Some days he even attempts to cooperate.

❧

THE SUN IS sinking when we arrive at the monastery, the north wind at our backs. The donkey and I have been sighted at a distance, and young Gregory runs out to meet us.

"Jordanes! Aren't you a sight for sore eyes! I knew you didn't eat the donkey. Now hurry, you've come just in time." He leads us up the path, calling out to the monks ahead of us.

"Look, brothers! It is Jordanes, returned with our wayward donkey."

The entire monastery gathers in the courtyard, buzzing with excitement.

"Someone retrieve Abba Gerasim!" Gregory says.

"That is our donkey! It is returned!" a voice calls.

"It couldn't possibly be our donkey," Abba Joseph snarks, standing in the doorway to the kitchens. "The lion made it a meal months ago."

Abba Poemen comes up behind him and speaks quietly but firmly. "It is our donkey, Abba. Heed the brand on its ear."

"Well, then, where has it been?"

"Perhaps it ran away, or perhaps it was taken by robbers," Abba Macarius offers. "Either way, it was certainly not eaten as we had supposed."

Abba Joseph looks as if he has swallowed a bug.

Abba Moses, an ancient and wiry man with nut-brown skin, kneels before me. "Forgive us,

Jordanes! Most honorable of beasts!"

Then I hear my favorite voice of all.

"Well done, your highness. Well done, Jordanes."

Gerasim breaks through the crowd, holding the hand of a particular hamadryas, my friend Astennu.

"Forgive us, father," says Abba Macarius, his eyes downcast. "You were right about the lion."

Gerasim smiles and gently squeezes the monk's shoulder. "Shall we give this overgrown puss his heart's desire, then?"

Abba Macarius dips his head, then turns and walks purposefully to me. He reaches out and lightly strokes my mane, and his hand does not tremble the slightest bit. One by one, the other monks approach me, touching me and speaking to me with affection and apology. The air fills with the freshness of sweet running water and the soughing of a misted breeze through shade-giving leaves. A hearty lion-purr rumbles through my chest, and I learn yet another of its secrets: that it is made out of the very substance of love.

Thus begins my acceptance.

The monks no longer fear me.

EIGHT

Gerasim

THE WEEKS AFTER my return are sweet and novel, filled with the frisson of new friendship. Everything is the same, and yet everything is different. My master's presence is like oil running down my head, softening and protecting, soothing and cleansing.

My return has loosed something imprisoned in the monks' hearts, something that feared to break free from the comfort of routine and prejudice. There is more laughter, more joy in the small moments. The oil of my master's peace runs throughout the monastery, and with my acceptance, ignites into a flame that illumines the entire cliffside. The eyes of the monks burn with love for each other and for all of creation, and the voices of their vespers echo the thunder on the mountain.

In these days, even the act of guarding the grazing donkey is charged with meaning, and I follow him gladly to the river and back. He is still stupid, but his obstinacy has mellowed in the peace of the lavra, and he does not tremble at my nearness anymore. He does not try to become more than what he is, and he is not particular by any stretch, but he refuses to be less than a good donkey. The monks smile at the slight change in his demeanor, and go about their tasks as if my presence renews their cenobitic vows.

"Silly lion, you know that it is not all about you."

Astennu's affectionate chiding breaks my

reverie, and I sneeze in response.

"What else could it be? I left in disgrace and have returned to love. This is what they call a miracle, is it not?"

"Of course it is, my lord. But there is more. Ask me what it was like while you were gone."

"Pah! It is a monastery. Nothing changes."

"I was not here at the monastery."

I cock my head in surprise. "Did you return to the savanna?"

"No. I traveled with Gerasim across wide waters."

The gaping mouth of a surprised lion would terrify all but the baboon doubled up in laughter before me.

"You truly are a prideful lion, Jordanes. Did you think life simply stopped when you left, holding its breath until you returned? Did you forget that yours is not the only story being told?"

There is no response to her questions that will allow me to preserve my dignity, so I merely twitch my tail. After a while, Astennu sits beside me and begins to pick the tangles from my mane. I rumble in contentment and smooth the hairs on her spine with my rough tongue, a wordless, but sincere, apology.

"Tell me of your journey, Astennu."

She weaves her words, and even though the river for which I was named is the largest water I have ever seen, I begin to see the great sea of her journey in my mind's eye. I can hear the lapping of the waves against the wood of the vessel, feel the lurching of the ground beneath her feet. Then she describes another sea, a sea of men and of words, of voices raised in counterpoint and harmony.

"There were many like our master, Jordanes. Men and women whose presence was autumn rain and starry skies. When they sang and spoke, I could almost see what the new creation will be like. But there were others, too, whose hunger for power was a wrongness that corrupted subtly—the way when Abba Poemen cooks his cabbages it can be mistaken for the smell of decay, or the way an overripe fruit in the bottom of the sack swells with sweet scent just before it bursts with worms."

"I do not understand. They were robbers, like the men who stole the donkey and the woman?"

"Not quite, Jordanes. Their wrongness was not so obvious, and so was much more dangerous. I was afraid, lion, afraid for the world in their hands. Were it not for the assurances of Gerasim and the glad confidence of the others, I would have resigned myself to hopelessness. But Gerasim promises me that the wrongness they can do is only temporary, whereas the rightness of Gerasim and his clear-eyed friends will last forever."

"Hamadryas, I do not understand most of what you say, but one thing you say is obvious to me: that the legacy of our master Gerasim will be for a thousand years."

We are quiet together as the sun sinks into its red rest.

"What does he teach you, Astennu? Why is he different for you than for me?"

Astennu drops her hands into her lap, inspecting them.

"He is different for me because you and I are different, lion. You were a natural lion who left his lands voluntarily; I am an unnatural beast who has known more men than baboons. You and Gerasim share a love that needs no words. For me, the words of men get in the way. I hear the rhythms of the myths of Thoth and Osiris, and I hear their echoes in the stories Gerasim tells. He untangles the strands for me, so that someday they may no longer bind me to men."

"You do not plan to stay here forever?" I ask, surprised. "Why would you ever want to leave?"

Astennu's brow wrinkles.

"I do not know the answer to that yet, Jordanes. I hope it will come to me before I am old."

❧

THE SUN CHASES the moon. He never tires, and he never catches his prey. Season follows season, and they pass in peace. My mane fades like grass in the winter as the years add their toll to our mortal frames.

Our master bends and withers, dried up by the desert sun, but his presence is sweeter day by day. When he is too tired to walk, I carry him upon my back. At night he rests his precious head against my soft flank, and my lion-purr lulls him to sleep. He wakes often in the night, soft songs on his lips.

I still carry water when it is needed, though other donkeys throughout the years have shared that labor. None have been quite as obstinate as that first beast, and have been glad of my protection, loath to stray. Never again have the monks feared me, though young initiates into the lavra have needed some convincing. Such circumstances crinkle Gerasim's aging face with laughter, his rheumy eyes brightening with delight.

I know when the final day has come, because even the abbas can smell the scent of water and roses. My master calls them to his side, one by one, and blesses each, scattering joy amidst their sorrow. We keep vigil throughout the night, the men, the baboon, and I, waiting for the hour of his departure. Finally, he closes his eyes. As his breath leaves his body for the last time, I watch the golden mist that rises with it. It lingers above his body like a small cloud until a shining hand parts the veil and reaches out towards it. In a sound like the small breeze after a storm, I hear a voice whisper, "Come." The golden mist winks away.

For the last time, I roar. It thunders forth with exultation and shakes the stones of the crags and caves.

They bury his body at the top of the cliff, and a sense of rightness seeps down from the place of his repose through the warren of men, spreading out onto the meadow below like spilled honey. In a scarlet wave of rapture, the anemone flowers burst into bloom, and the thrushes explode into paschal arias.

I lay my silvered mane upon his grave and close my eyes. Though his days have ended, I cannot but follow my master still.

The sun and the moon continue their chase across the sky, and though the abbas bring me bread and dates, I live only on the love of my master. My eyes grow dim.

"Is it grief that breaks you, Jordanes?" Astennu asks me, her voice strained with concern. She sits beside me, stroking my mane. I lift my head and look at her, a lovely baboon female in the prime of her life, and I wonder what keeps her at the monastery still.

"It is not grief, Astennu, nor fear. Our master is not far, and I can feel his presence hidden just behind the veil."

Her simian face crumples. "I am glad for you, my lord, though I cannot sense such things."

"You are not yet near the borders of life, hamadryas. I have lived a full term for a lion, and I will not cease following the man who made me the lion Jordanes. It is meet and right."

She nods in agreement, though she continues to mourn quietly.

It is the last time we speak, though Astennu does not leave my side.

Finally, I feel the weight of the bright hand I have longed for, the sound of the voice from the golden cloud.

"Come, Jordanes, into your rest."

And so ends my earthly life.

NINE

The Baboon with the Moon on Her Head

 HEY BURIED THE lion beside his master, and they sang him a funeral song.

They buried my friends beneath the hill.

I fear they buried my words with them.

The loss of Gerasim and Jordanes wounds my heart in ways I did not expect, though I had tried to pray for wisdom and readiness. I have neither one—only the deep well of grief that drips sour in the pit of my stomach.

I spend the days upon the cliff, looking out on the river, and the nights in the chapel, curled up in front of the holy ox and ass. Sometimes I hide myself in the church, perched at the top of the support column where the rock makes natural hand- and footholds. It is there that young Gregory, now neither young nor called Gregory any longer, finds me.

"Astennu, are you up there?"

In a moment of hope, I try to answer him. "I am here, Abba Thomas, but I am alone." The sound of my voice is a croon of mourning.

"Come on down, old girl. I've got some dates for you."

The abba hears only the hooting of a baboon. I do not go down to him.

Instead I hold on to the memory of Gerasim's whispered voice, heard in the corners of my ears as Jordanes slipped away, and I cling to the comfort of knowing that they are together. But even though the monks are kind to me, setting out food and allowing me free rein of the lavra, I am utterly alone again, for none of them hears me. And if they cannot hear me, can they really know me?

I pass the time by recalling the many conversations that I had with the man who understood me and spoke with me and helped me become myself. Remembering his voice makes him feel near again, and I wonder at how I never missed the temple men or the kitchen girl in this way, even after they were taken by the maneater or fled to their city. They were never as foul and stinking as Jordanes claimed men could be, but neither did they shed the scent of water and honey like my master. I pestered Gerasim about it repeatedly, trying to make sense of my past.

"Was I reared by evil men, then, Gerasim? If they followed the old ways and the old gods?"

He smiled at me then, his laughing, peaceful smile, and asked, "What do you know of your namesake?"

"I know that Astennu was a servant of the lord of silence and the thrice-great god of hidden knowledge. Only they were but rumors of the true thrice-great and the still small voice."

"Yes—Astennu the servant, the scribe of Thoth the terrible and Osiris the royal shepherd. It is easy to love the old stories, puzzles and secret mysteries that hint at the glories to come. It is not difficult to see the scales of Osiris to be a prophecy of the Last Judgment. Do you see?"

I nodded slowly.

"Think on it, dear one. When the risen god weighs the hearts of men against a feather, it is Astennu who records his verdict in the annals of eternity, creating with his words a language of redemption and damnation. It is a very fitting name for you, my observer, for how else would you describe the gift you share with Jordanes?"

"Yes, an observer," I interrupted, "An outsider. I do not understand why I do not belong to you the way Jordanes does."

"Because you are not Jordanes!" he laughed. "Jordanes the lion is a king, not a philosopher, and the best kings are the truest servants of all.

But it is good that I have a hamadryas, too, to play with words and hold my accounts up to the light of the truth, the way all good scribes do. Your story is a secret hand of God, Astennu, an in-breaking of the glory to come into the life of a simple baboon.

"Remember, you will live longer than I will. You must decide what to do with the rest of your story when the time comes."

I ignored the implication and circled back to the beginning. "But what of the temple men?"

"What of them?"

"Were they wicked?"

"You tell me, baboon. You have met all kinds of life over the years. Most creatures must be only what they are; particular beasts like you and Jordanes are possible, but rare. It is the blessing and curse of humankind to be forced to choose between being more than or less than what we are in every moment of our lives. For us there is no middle way. So, tell me, Astennu. Were you reared by less-than-humans?"

I looked inward at the scrolls of memory. "It is hard to tell, master. Many had barely begun to choose either way. They were nothing like you, and I did not know love then."

"Ah! But not choosing is a choice, just a slow one."

"But I did know kindness, master. They were not the rancid things Jordanes despises."

"Then there is hope, hamadryas. With beasts and with humans, with all of creation, there is always hope."

And after speaking with him, I always knew that to be true.

Gerasim made me as ready for the moment of decision as it was possible to be, but when I finally find myself standing at the bank of the river and looking back up at the lavra shining white in the sun, I almost run back to the monks and the safe rhythms of their choosing.

Instead, I lope into the flowered meadow and begin to retrace the steps of my journey from so long ago. I must go even further back than my fated meeting with Jordanes, to the place where my own tale began, to the old temple in the wilds, and the journey takes many uneventful desert days. When I arrive, I find the cool stone temple in utter ruin, with shrubs growing in the cracked mortar and a nest of snakes in the crumbling kitchen. The surrounding outbuildings have been buffeted by the khamaseen winds of many seasons, and none are left standing beneath the drifts of dust and sand. It was a relic even when the temple men still lived here; now it is only the ghost of a forgotten past.

I pluck a locust from the grass and watch the desert devour my youth.

A rustle in the brush behind me reveals a young hamadryas female, curious and investigating. She is the first of my kind I have seen in years upon years, for no band of baboons had ever lived near the lavra, and my heart begins to pound. Will she speak to me, changed as I am by the scents of holy man and lion? Will I even be capable of a response?

You are hamadryas, she signals to me.

I am.

Where is your troop?

They are gone.

She does not look me straight in the eye, but glances off to one side or the other. My hands tremble, and I smooth the fine hairs on my knuckles to still them.

Come. Come to mine.

It is a terrifying thought—to join a band—but one that has haunted me for years. How will I bear it—to be more than hamadryas among all the others, who are merely baboons?

But then, how can I not? In order to be more than hamadryas, I must also be fully hamadryas, drinking the cup to its last drop. I have lived among men and not been human. I must know what it means to live among my own kind.

So I follow the female to her family.

IT IS JARRING, at first, never to speak except in the body and eye and chemical languages of beasts. But I fall into the rhythm and companionship of life with other baboons, and this kind of silence is not as lonely as being among men without Gerasim and Jordanes. It is not long before I am with child.

Such a common thing for other baboons is a great mystery to me.

In the deluge of a life-giving winter rain, I give life to a daughter, and the magnitude of the moment forces words back up from my heart, like a spring undammed. Her tiny body nestles against my breast, her fingers entwined in my fur, and my soul sings as it did when I clung to the column of the church and bathed in lyric. The need to speak and to sing is urgent, though I do not know how I will ever tell it all. For, having introduced her to the sun and sky and rain and wind, how can I bear to not teach her all of the other mysteries I have touched? How can I not hope for her a life with a name?

I will teach her the true Way of the world, and I will teach her to speak.

And so I begin, long fingers entwined with tiny ones, face to face.

"I was a solitary baboon, taken from my band as an infant and raised as a temple monkey by men who preserved the worship of the ibis-headed god. I was nurtured on the knee of a storyteller, who sang me the songs of his people and taught me their rhythms and rhymes. My life's tale is tangled with the story of a lion who was a king and a servant, and the story of the holy man who gave us names. They were my friends, which is a man-word for one who helps you become particular.

"I am your mother, and your friend, so I will tell you all that I've known, so that you, too, my beautiful child, may find your name and be known."

As the words begin to flow, I discover I will not be content to share speech and being only with my child. I am Astennu, particular and named, observer and scribe, hamadyras and more than hamadryas, and now it is time to spin the tale of my witness. For this story is good news—and it is meant for all creatures great and small.

THE END

AURA E. WOLFE is the author of the beloved picture book *Sasha and the Dragon* (Ancient Faith Publishing, 2017). A wide-eyed nature lover her entire life, Laura has a bachelor of science degree in biology with a minor in philosophy, and she still thinks the best place to read a good novel is halfway up a tree. She and her family are members of St. Paul Antiochian Orthodox Church in Emmaus, Pennsylvania.

Ancient Faith Publishing hopes you have enjoyed and benefited from this book. The proceeds from the sales of our books only partially cover the costs of operating our nonprofit ministry—which includes both the work of **Ancient Faith Publishing** and the work of **Ancient Faith Radio**. Your financial support makes it possible to continue this ministry both in print and online. Donations are tax deductible and can be made at **www.ancientfaith.com**.

To view our other publications,
please visit our website:
store.ancientfaith.com

 **ANCIENT FAITH RADIO**

Bringing you Orthodox Christian music,
readings, prayers, teaching, and podcasts
24 hours a day since 2004 at
www.ancientfaith.com

Lightning Source UK Ltd.
Milton Keynes UK
UKHW021452290421
382821UK00020B/725